Beast Quest®

OKIRA
THE CRUSHER

BY ADAM BLADE

ORCHARD

WELCOME TO

Beast
Quest

Collect the special coins in this book.
You will earn one gold coin for
every chapter you read.

Once you have finished all the chapters,
find out what to do with your gold coins at
the back of the book.

With special thanks to Tabitha Jones

For Scott, Alfie and Ferneé Gilchrist

www.beast-quest.com

ORCHARD BOOKS

First published in Great Britain in 2017 by The Watts Publishing Group

1 3 5 7 9 10 8 6 4 2

Text © 2017 Beast Quest Limited.
Cover and inside illustrations by Steve Sims
© Beast Quest Limited 2017

Beast Quest is a registered trademark of Beast Quest Limited
Series created by Beast Quest Limited, London

A CIP catalogue record for this book is available from the British Library.

ISBN 978 1 40834 323 4

Printed in Great Britain

The paper and board used in this book are made from wood from responsible sources

Orchard Books
An imprint of Hachette Children's Group
Part of The Watts Publishing Group Limited
Carmelite House, 50 Victoria Embankment, London EC4Y 0DZ

An Hachette UK Company
www.hachette.co.uk
www.hachettechildrens.co.uk

CONTENTS

1. THE FOREST OF THE LOST   11
2. THE TRAPPED WIZARD   27
3. THE DEAD FORTRESS   39
4. NO WAY IN   53
5. A DEADLY JUMP   67
6. THE BEAST AWAKENS   81
7. THE WIZARD'S STAFF   101
8. THE QUEST CONTINUES   115

They thought I was dead, but death is not always the end.

My body was consumed in Ferno's dragon-fire, though that pain is a distant memory now. I have been trapped in this place – this Isle of Ghosts – for too long. It is time for me to remind my old enemies of my power.

The boundary between the realm of spirits and the realm of the living is like a thick castle wall – unbreakable by force or magic. But every castle has its weakness – someone on the inside who can lower the drawbridge. And I have found him. A weak wizard, but strong enough to do my bidding.

Hear me, Berric! Heed my summons. Open the way for me to return, and I will show Avantia that Evil like mine is impossible to kill.

Malvel

THE FOREST OF THE LOST

Tom staggered through the endless reeking marshland, his back bent and his eyes to the ground. Mud sucked at his boots with each step and his sword and shield weighed him down. He glanced up to see Elenna ahead of him, outlined against the dull red sky of the Isle of

Ghosts. She turned and frowned at him, anxiously.

"Why don't we stop for a bit?" she said.

Tom shook his head. "We have to find Malvel," he said hoarsely. Since the ghost of the Dark Wizard had drained his life force, Tom had felt a coldness inside him, sapping away his strength. But he had to go on. Malvel had the Amulet of Avantia. That meant he only needed a key from a Ghost Beast, and he'd be able to return home.

And then he'll be unstoppable...

Suddenly, a strange mist swirled up from the mud ahead of them, like tendrils of smoke caught in an eddy.

The mist thickened into a twisting column, quickly settling into a familiar figure – a tall man with a golden beard and hair swept back from a noble face.

"Father!" Tom gasped.

Taladon's eyes were filled with pity. "Malvel will not rest until he has destroyed you, my son," he said. "And if you linger here too long, the ghost world will take you completely. Some Quests are unwinnable. There is no shame in admitting that."

Tom made himself stand tall. "It's not about shame, Father," he said. "I swore to protect Avantia from Evil. I can't let Malvel return there."

Taladon bowed his head. When he lifted his eyes, Tom felt some of his strength return at the pride he saw in his father's gaze. "You are right, son," Taladon said. "I wish I could fight this battle in your place. Instead, all I can offer is guidance."

Taladon pointed towards the dark treeline on the horizon. "The next stage of your Quest lies to the east. You must navigate the Forest of the Lost – a cursed place full of stranded spirits. Beyond the forest you will find a fortress that Malvel

has taken as his own – a stronghold from which he can subdue the Beasts of this land, ready to invade Avantia. Be careful, Tom. Malvel burns for revenge. He will show no mercy."

Tom balled his fists. "I have beaten Malvel before. I will beat him again."

Taladon nodded gravely. "I hope you are right." Before Tom could speak again, Taladon dissolved into shreds of mist that seeped into the earth.

"To the Forest of the Lost it is, then," Tom said, breaking into a run, Elenna at his side. Taladon's words had stirred a fierce determination inside him. As they ran over the barren plains, he let the rasp of his breath and the thud of his boots on the ground fill his mind.

Before long, the treeline loomed darkly before them. Gnarled and twisted trunks, leafless and blackened, rose from the grey, dry earth. Crows squawked at their approach and small shadows scurried between the trunks, making a chill creep down Tom's spine. Beside him, Elenna eyed the silver-black wood of the trees with a wary, almost frightened look. The cracked bark looked brittle and scorched, and the smell of stale smoke hung in the air. Tom felt a rush of sympathy for his friend. Elenna had lost both parents in a forest blaze – if she could be said to fear anything, it was fire.

"I'll understand if you can't go on," said Tom.

Elenna shivered, then raised her chin. Her eyes glittered fiercely in the half dark. "This fire burned out long ago," she said. "And even if it were burning now, I wouldn't leave you to face this battle alone."

Blackened twigs crunched beneath their boots as they trudged between the trees. Though the air was still, branches creaked and groaned overhead. From all around them, Tom could hear a whispering rustle, like the sound of leaves in the breeze, though every branch was bare.

Within it, Tom caught snatches of words.

"The voices of spirits," said Elenna, her face pale.

As they went on, the whispers grew louder, mixed with stifled laughter and muffled sobs. Elenna shivered and glanced over her shoulder, and Tom couldn't help doing the same.

He squinted ahead through shadows. At first, he saw nothing, but then he glimpsed what looked almost like features set into the trunks. He blinked, wondering if his eyes were playing tricks on him. With a sharp tug of heart-stopping horror, he realised they were not.

"The trees have faces!" he hissed,

catching Elenna's sleeve. They
edged forward to a huge black oak.
The ridges in the bark formed the
unmistakable shape of a crooked

nose. Below the nose, a splintered hole gaped wide like a mouth wailing in grief. Above, a pair of dark eyes seemed to gaze at them.

Tom shivered.

"Trapped souls," Elenna whispered, echoing Taladon's words.

They crept on in silence. Branches with long, twiggy fingers pulled at Tom's hair and clothes as he passed beneath them.

Elenna stopped suddenly, her head tipped to one side as if listening hard. "Can you hear that?" she said.

Tom listened, hearing nothing but the sound of their own breathing, and a faint rustling.

"Mother?" Elenna hissed. Her

eyes widened suddenly. "Father!"
She leapt into a run, dashing wildly
through the trees.

"Elenna! Stop!" Tom called. But
she crashed onwards through the
branches, quickly moving out of
sight.

As Tom ran after her, his foot
caught in a tree root, and he fell.
He tried to stand, but the root had
somehow coiled about his ankle,
holding him fast. A rasping, hissing
sound rose up all around him,
making his scalp tingle with fear.
The ashy ground shifted. Snaking,
hairy roots broke the surface, groping
blindly upwards. One wormed
towards Tom's wrist. He gasped and

drew back his arm, then kicked his leg, trying to free his ankle.

Suddenly, a wrenching, creaking sound filled the air. Tom's stomach clenched in horror as an ugly, twisted mouth split open in the sooty wood of a trunk.

He scrabbled in the dirt, desperately trying to escape the clutching tendrils. As he reached for his sword, the root around his ankle jerked sharply upwards, yanking him into the air. The blood rushed to his head as he dangled upside down. He made a swipe for his sword as it slid from its scabbard, but missed. The blade plunged and landed point first in the ground.

The root lifted Tom towards the
dark, jagged mouth until he was
hanging over it. A hungry rumble

bubbled up from the hole in the trunk as it opened wider.

Wide enough to swallow him whole.

THE TRAPPED WIZARD

Tom reached up with a great effort, bent double and grabbed hold of the woody tendril around his ankle. The root jerked, lashing him from side to side and making his vision blur. Calling on the strength of his golden breastplate, he let out a roar and yanked at the root, tearing it in two.

He flew through the air, crashing through dry branches.

Thud!

He hit the ground, and lay still for a moment, catching his breath. But he could already hear more roots slithering all around him. Something shifted beneath his back, and he leapt to his feet. His sword poked up from the dirt nearby, a root worming towards it. Tom snatched up the weapon and ran through the gloom. Pale tendrils groped across the forest floor from every angle, creeping over each other in a vile tangle. They snapped at his feet and Tom leapt and hopped, slashing at them with his sword. He heard a cry

to his left, high and wild with terror.
Elenna!

Tom dived through the dense
knotted branches towards the sound.
And there she was, his friend, lying
on her back, sliding away from him
towards a jagged-edged mouth in
a tree, a root wrapped tight around

her waist.

I'll never reach her in time...

Tom gripped his shield by the rim, flexed his wrist and threw. The disc of wood spun though the air. *Smack!* It lodged in the tree's open mouth, blocking the hole. Elenna braced her feet against the shield and bucked her body, wriggling to get free.

"Help!" she gasped. Tom raced to her side and hacked at the root, chopping it in two. The severed halves rippled away and Elenna scrambled up, pale and shaking.

"Thank you," she said, just as the tree spat out Tom's shield.

Tom grabbed it. "Keep moving, Elenna," he said. "This forest doesn't want us to leave!"

They raced on through the wood, dodging groping, clutching roots. Finally, they burst into a clearing and pulled to a stop, panting. The dusky space was overshadowed by ancient-looking trees but was smooth underfoot, with no sign of the man-eating roots.

"I'm sorry I ran off," Elenna said between gasps. "I thought I heard my parents calling. I thought maybe their spirits were trapped in the trees here…" She closed her eyes and swallowed hard. "Do you think it was one of Malvel's tricks?"

"Perhaps," came a deep, rumbling voice from behind them, making

them jump. Tom spun, his sword
raised, to see a huge tree, leafless
and gnarled with age. A sorrowful

but kindly face, the size of a normal person's, peered at them from the trunk. It had bushy brows, a broad, straight nose and a long moustache. "There's no way of knowing," the tree went on, "not in the Forest of the Lost."

Tom let his sword fall. He and Elenna peered closely at the strange face. The dark hollows of its eyes seemed softer and more human than those of the other trees. Its mouth, half hidden by the long moustache, wore a sad smile. Long hair, like silvery moss sprouted from above the face and trailed all the way to the ground.

"Who are you?" Tom asked.

The tree sighed. "Now, I am no one. But I was once a great and powerful wizard, Kato. I lived in a realm called Gorgonia, though I doubt you will have heard of it."

Tom frowned. "I know it all too well," he said. "My greatest enemy once ruled there. A Dark Wizard named Malvel."

The face in the tree looked stern for a moment. "It was he who stole my place in Gorgonia," the wizard said, "more than thirty years ago. He banished me here to the Isle of Ghosts. I made a home in the Dead Fortress with the ogre Okira until Malvel showed up again. He cast a spell on the Good Beast, turning him to stone, then forced me from my home and into the forest. In my haste, I was snatched up by this tree. I have been trapped ever since."

"I could cut you free,"Tom said. "We could face Malvel together. If you fight with me, I'll do all I can to return you to your homeland."

Kato knotted his bushy brows, deep in thought. He nodded. "Free me," he said. "And I will help you all I can. But I fear I have been trapped on this island too long to return home. I am a ghost now."

Tom felt suddenly cold. He looked at his wrist, where Malvel had grabbed him, sucking out some of his life force. The lower arm had turned slightly faded, his veins standing out beneath the skin. *We could become trapped here too.* But

he took a deep breath, pushing his
fear deep down inside himself.

"I'm not leaving here until I've
stopped Malvel, once and for all," he
said. Then he lifted his sword and
swung it at the ancient tree that
trapped the wizard.

THE DEAD
FORTRESS

Thunk! Tom's blade glanced off the blackened trunk, barely leaving a mark.

"This wood is harder than rock!" he said.

"Just free my arm," Kato answered. "Then I can use my magic."

Tom nodded. To one side of the

tree, he could just make out the long, narrow shape of a limb, outlined in the singed bark. He drew back his sword, aiming next to it.

Thud! A shallow groove scored the trunk. Channelling all the power of the golden breastplate, Tom swung again. The wood splintered. Kato winced.

"Are you all right?" Elenna asked, peering anxiously at the wizard's face.

"Keep going," Kato answered. Tom hacked again and again at the tree. Sooty chips fell away, littering the forest floor. Finally, the wizard's arm and hand stood proud of the tree, like a half-finished carving. Tom stepped back, and wiped the sweat from his brow.

"Can you move?" he asked.

Kato frowned, then his fingers flexed slowly and he lifted his robed arm. "Stand back," the wizard said. Kato made a ball with his fist, shook it twice, then opened it. A flash of amber light, like the glare of a low sun on a winter's day, blinded Tom for a moment. When he could see again, he found Kato standing before him, leaning on a knobbly staff. A huge hole, roughly the shape of the wizard, gaped darkly in the tree behind him, but it was closing fast, like a wound healing with magical speed.

Kato flexed his shoulders and straightened his back, grimacing. He shook clouds of black dust from his cloak, revealing bright colours underneath. Though Kato's long dark hair and moustache were streaked with grey, his black eyes shone fiercely. A red cloak, decorated with golden runes, fell in folds from his shoulders. Kato cracked his neck, then let out a satisfied sigh.

"That's better!" he said.

"Can you lead us to the fortress?" Tom asked.

Kato smiled, his eyes twinkling as he raised his staff. "It would be my pleasure," he said. The wizard

turned sharply, cloak swirling behind him, and he led Tom and Elenna from the clearing. As soon as they stepped back beneath the scorched trees, the earth stirred. With a slithering hiss, buried roots whipped up at their feet. Tom sliced the tendrils with his sword as Elenna danced lightly through the clutching mass, pinning them with arrows fired from her bow.

Kato growled. "It's time to show the Forest of the Lost what a true Wizard of Gorgonia can do." He turned to Elenna. "Give me one of your arrows. These trees fear one thing only." Elenna drew an arrow from her quiver and handed it to the wizard, who held it aloft and focussed his black eyes on the tip. The arrow glowed under the wizard's gaze, then burst into spitting flames.

Kato passed the burning arrow to Elenna, who held it up, firelight flickering off her haunted face. Her jaw clenched. "I can't be afraid for ever. Let's set this forest alight." She fitted it to her bow, then narrowed her eyes, focussing on a tall, straight trunk nearby. *Fizz!* The flaming shaft hit the trunk, then – *Whumph!* – the whole tree went up like a pile of rags soaked with oil. Tom put up his arms to shield his face from the scorching heat.

The flames crackled and roared, reaching into the sky. Nearby trees creaked and hissed, drawing their branches back from the flames. Pale roots shrank away, disappearing beneath the soil. In only a few blistering heartbeats the fire died, leaving nothing of the tree but a crooked stump smoking gently in the sudden quiet.

Elenna turned to Kato, wide-eyed with surprise, but grinning. "It worked! The roots are scared of us."

"Not bad for someone who's been trapped in a tree for thirty years, eh?" Kato said.

Tom grinned too. Something about the wizard's sharp gaze and bright smile reminded him of Aduro. It was good to have magic back on their side.

The three of them started off again through the silent forest. Although Tom's skin prickled with the uneasy sense of watchful eyes on them, he saw no more faces in the trees, and the roots stayed firmly buried. They travelled quickly, and before long the black trees began to thin out. Finally, Tom, Elenna and Kato passed from beneath the last few boughs and found themselves at the edge of a wide, flat plain of barren rock, the same brownish red as the sky.

In the distance, a colossal wall rose up, blank and featureless, built from blocks of dull grey stone. It curved around a fortress, hiding all but four square towers topped with strange, hunched shapes.

Tom, Elenna and Kato strode over the uneven ground for what seemed like hours – but with no sun or moon to mark the time, it was impossible to say. Although Kato walked with his shoulders square and his head held high, Tom noticed that sweat beaded the wizard's forehead, and his face looked pinched and grey.

"Are you all right?" Elenna asked the wizard.

"Never better!" Kato said. But as they continued over the dusty plain, the lines on his face seemed to deepen, and his eyes took on a feverish gleam.

Soon Tom could make out the shapes on the fortress towers – four huge stone hounds, frozen mid-leap, their jaws open. Beneath them,

narrow windows in the towers
peered out like evil eyes.

With no shelter or camouflage to
hide them, Tom felt as exposed as a

mouse in the flight path of an owl. He kept glancing up, expecting to see archers on the wall, or some other threat awaiting them.

They stopped at the edge of a wide, dark moat that reflected the unchanging, sunless sky, like a pool of blood. A wooden drawbridge stood raised against the wall on the other side.

"Welcome to the Dead Fortress," Kato said.

NO WAY IN

Tom gazed at the structure. Snakes
of dread squirmed in the pit of his
stomach.

There was no sign of Malvel, but
his father had sent them this way.
We can't be too careful...

"How do we get in?" Tom said.

Kato frowned. "As you might
expect, the fortress has excellent

defences. It is not designed to let anyone in."

Elenna looked doubtfully at the dank water of the moat. A greasy film covered its surface and an eggy stink rose from it, so strong it made Tom's eyes water.

"I suppose we could swim?" she said uncertainly.

"I wouldn't try it if I were you," Kato said. He clicked his fingers. A pebble at the edge of the moat rattled and lifted into the air. It hovered above the water, then fell, disappearing with a plop. The black water fizzed. A foam of yellow bubbles rose to the surface, giving off acrid smoke.

Tom's stomach sank. "Acid," he said.

"Indeed," Kato answered. Suddenly a loud *clunk* followed by a metallic rattle echoed across the moat. The vast wooden drawbridge opposite began to lower on rusty chains, gradually revealing a huge, open archway in the wall. Beyond the arch, Tom could just make out a gloomy courtyard. "Malvel's daring us to cross," he said.

Kato frowned. "Then we can be sure he'll have planned a warm welcome."

Elenna took her bow from her back. "Whatever his plans, we have to go on," she said. "We can't defeat him from out here."

Tom nodded. He lifted his sword and stepped warily on to the bridge, his footsteps ringing hollowly. Kato and Elenna stepped to his side.

He peered hard into the dusky open space beyond the archway. Nothing stirred.

Suddenly a mighty crash tore through the dim air, sending a shock of adrenaline up Tom's spine. At his side, Kato brandished his staff and Elenna raised her bow. The drawbridge jumped beneath Tom's feet as another thunderous crash rang out, then a third. A low, bloodcurdling growl filled the air, making the hair on Tom's arms stand on end.

"That doesn't sound good," Elenna

hissed, aiming her bow through the archway.

The growl rose to an angry snarl and four stone hounds the size of horses slouched through the arch, standing shoulder to shoulder at the far end of the bridge. Tom recognised the broad heads, narrowed eyes and blunt snouts. "They're the statues from the towers," he said. Gargoyles, brought to life by Evil magic. The four creatures drew back their lips, revealing sharp, curved teeth.

"I'll deal with them," Kato cried, leaping past Tom, his cloak whipping behind him. He lifted his staff, sending a ball of golden energy whizzing towards the hounds. *Crack!*

The ball exploded into a starburst of sparks against one creature's flank, throwing it into the moat with a strangled yelp. Kato fired a second bolt. *Boom!* Another hound flew sideways in a flare of yellow flames. The acid fizzed as the creatures flailed, their stone features dissolving. Before long, only yellow foam remained.

The two hounds still on the bridge stood snarling, their hackles raised, eyeing Kato with a mixture of fury and fear. The wizard fired another blast, but this one was smaller and moved more slowly through the air. The dogs split apart, and the ball of magic flew between them, exploding

against the bridge. Kato lifted his staff once more, but Tom could see the wizard's body shaking. Kato fired two more bolts, but both fizzled out in the air before reaching their mark.

Kato clutched his chest. "Malvel's close," the wizard gasped. "He's draining my strength!" He sank to his knees, shuddering for breath.

The two hounds on the bridge lowered their heads and glared, like bulls ready to charge. Tom and Elenna sprang forward to stand before the wizard. Elenna fired an arrow but it pinged off a stone snout without leaving a mark. The monster shook his head, then thundered towards her with a snarl, shaking the bridge beneath Tom's feet.

Tom drew back his shield and flung himself into the creature's path. Using his shield like a battering ram, he slammed the wood into the stone dog's flank. The blow sent the creature barrelling off the bridge. *Splash!* Acid erupted from the moat, spattering the bridge, leaving smoking holes.

"Tom! Look out!" Elenna cried. Tom glanced up to see the final stone hound spring. He swung his sword and met the creature's attack with all his strength, slamming the flat of his blade across its muzzle. His arm and shoulder exploded

with pain and he flew backwards
through the air. Tom landed heavily
on his back, cracking his head
against the drawbridge. Lights burst

before Tom's eyes and he lay dazed, clutching his arm and gasping with pain.

"Tom!" Elenna screamed. Tom shook his head and tried to focus his vision. His heart jolted as he saw the hound bound towards him again, then pounce through the air – a vast weight of stone, bristling with claws and teeth. Before his muddled senses could react, strong hands grabbed his shoulders and yanked, pulling him from the gargoyle's path.

Elenna!

Tom scrambled up beside her. The hound's forepaws smashed through the acid-weakened planks of the bridge, where Tom had been lying.

The stone creature bucked and scrabbled at the wood, dislodging more planks and sending them plunging into the acid waters. Finally, the gargoyle heaved itself free, leaving a huge, jagged gap in the bridge. Cracks spread through the timber. Groans and creaks rose from beneath Tom's feet. The bridge trembled then lurched.

"The bridge is going to collapse!" yelled Elenna.

1

A DEADLY JUMP

The gargoyle turned and raced back into the fortress, as the bridge began to break apart.

"Run!" Tom shouted.

They raced back over the quaking bridge, the splash and hiss of wood plunging into acid, loud beneath them. Kato knelt where Tom had left him, his head bent as if too heavy to lift. Tom and Elenna each grabbed one of the wizard's arms, then sped on, half running, half staggering, dragging Kato towards the bank.

With a deafening splitting sound, the bridge fell away under them. Tom leapt just in time, pulling Kato with him on to the bank, but he heard a shout at his side. He turned to see Elenna disappearing in a pile of wooden planks.

"No!" Tom shouted.

A fountain of acid rose up as the timbers fell into the moat. Tom's stomach clenched in panic. Then he saw fingers curled around the broken end of the bridge.

"I can't hold myself!" Elenna

shouted. Her fingers slipped...

Tom dived forward, landing on his
stomach and reaching down. His
hand gripped hold of Elenna's wrist.
He looked down at her, hanging over
the bubbling lake of acid.

"Pull me up!" she shouted.

Tom heaved, pulling her over the lip so she sprawled on the ground beside him.

"Thank you," she gasped.

Kato stood brushing the dust from his tattered cloak. The wizard still looked pale, but his eyes were stern. Beyond him, planks of wood bobbed and spun in the moat, fizzing as they dwindled to nothing. On the far bank, a single stone gargoyle paced backwards and forwards in the archway, eyeing them darkly. Above it, and to either side, towered the high walls of the fortress.

"How do we get in now?" Elenna asked.

Tom scanned the stone barrier,

biting his lip.

"Even using the power of my golden boots, I don't think I can get all three of us across," he said. He turned to Kato. "You are sick," Tom said. "If you stay here, I think I can get Elenna and myself to the top of the wall."

Kato smiled shakily. "And miss all the fun? No. I'll make my own way." He closed his eyes and took a deep breath, as if summoning his strength, then pointed his staff towards the fortress wall. With a gentle *pop*, the wizard vanished. A moment later he appeared at the top of the wall, outlined against the dull red sky. Tom saw the wizard sway, then stagger. Elenna gasped as Kato teetered right on the edge of the wall. *He's going to fall!*

But somehow Kato managed to catch his balance. He lifted a hand. "I'm fine!" the wizard called, before sinking to his knees.

Tom turned to Elenna and grinned. "Are you ready?" he asked.

Elenna returned his grin. "I think so," she said, and grabbed hold of his shield.

Tom called on the power of his golden boots. He bent his knees and leapt, focussing on the stretch of wall beside Kato. They soared up over the moat.

But as they neared the top of the

wall, Tom felt them slowing. *We're not going to make it!* Desperately, he called on the power of his golden breastplate and hurled Elenna up. She landed lightly on the wall beside Kato, but Tom realised that he was going to fall well short. His stomach flipped as the grey stone brickwork rushed past before him. He groped frantically for the wall, his feet pumping the air and his arms outstretched… *Yes!* He just managed to catch the edge of a stone brick with one hand. He reached up with his other hand, fingers finding another hold. As his feet scrabbled for a grip, chips of stone skittered down to fizz in the moat far below. When Tom finally felt secure, he let out a breath. "Phew!" He took another moment to settle his nerves, then climbed up to join Elenna and Kato.

Elenna shot him a shaky smile. "I thought I'd lost you there for a moment!" she said.

Tom found Kato gnawing at his lip with worry. Though the wizard seemed to have regained some of his strength, his face still looked drawn and grey. He pointed down into the courtyard, overshadowed by the vast keep, its four square towers now empty of hounds. "Okira," Kato said.

A colossal stone ogre slouched against a tower, its chin resting on its knees. The Beast's vast shoulders bulged with muscles, and its massive fists looked big enough to punch through the walls. A long chain, also made of stone, reached from a manacle about the ogre's wrist to an iron spike embedded in the brickwork of the tower.

"Okira and I lived here together for years," Kato said. "Though young and wild, the Good Beast was fiercely loyal. But then Malvel took even Okira's friendship from me."

Malvel's sneering voice suddenly rang out across the courtyard, loud and clear and filled with spite. "Oh, please, spare us the sob story!" he said, stepping out from a dark doorway in the keep. Even from this distance, Malvel looked healthier

than when Tom had last seen him only days before. His body was more solid, the colour returned to his skin.

"He's not a ghost any more!" said Tom.

The Dark Wizard straightened, clutching his staff at his side. "And I have you to thank for that," said Malvel. "Your life force has made me strong. Soon all Avantia will bow before me."

1

THE BEAST AWAKENS

Malvel pointed his staff at Kato. "You should have stayed in the Forest of the Lost, weakling." He jabbed his staff at the ogre. "But if you miss your pet so much, why don't you come down here and join him?"

"Release him from your spell!"

Kato shouted.

Malvel leered. "I don't think so. Maybe if you two are such good friends, I can make you even closer!"

Tom lifted his sword and shield, ready for whatever evil Malvel sent their way. Elenna set an arrow to her bow and Kato brandished his own staff. But, far below them, Malvel simply smiled and opened his hand, as if releasing a fly. A flapping shadow, like a misshapen bat, flew from the wizard's palm, growing fast as it sped towards them. Elenna released her arrow, but it fizzed straight through the shadow and clattered into the courtyard far below. The dark, flapping shape loomed closer, twisting and stretching, like a ragged patch of night, blotting their view. Kato fired an orange bolt from the tip of his staff, but it vanished like a torch plunged into water when it hit the growing shadow.

The inky shape crested the wall and Tom threw up his shield, hoping to slam the thing aside, but his shield met no resistance and he stumbled, almost toppling from the wall. Kato let out an anguished cry as the dark blot wrapped around him, snatching him up. Tom and Elenna both tried to grab for the wizard, but he was torn from their

grip with tremendous force. Malvel
made a twisting gesture with his
hand.

The shadow shot across the
courtyard, carrying the struggling

wizard. Tom could see him screaming silently as his body warped and bulged within the black cloud. Malvel's face twisted with spite and he made one final flinging gesture, then closed his fist. The vast shadow slammed into Okira's bent form, then vanished. Tom gasped with horror. Kato was gone.

"Where did he go?" Elenna cried. "He can't be dead..."

Tom glared down at Malvel. "Whatever you've done to Kato," he cried, "you won't get away with it!" Tom called on the power of Arcta's eagle feather, which allowed him to glide through the air. "Cling on!" he told Elenna. She gripped Tom's arm and he leapt from the wall, lifting his shield overhead like a sail.

Malvel smiled. "You're making this far too easy," he said, pointing the tip of his staff at Tom and Elenna. A terrific whooshing sound filled the air, then Tom felt a fierce wind hit, almost tearing the shield from his hands. He tried to ride the gust, but the wind whipped around him, throwing them back. *Smack!* The edge of his shield clipped the wall, sending them into a downwards spin.

"Hang on!" Tom shouted, as the whirling courtyard sped up to meet them.

They landed in a tangle of limbs

and scrambled up. Tom could feel throbbing pain all over his body, and Elenna winced, clutching her arm. The wind had died as quickly as it started, but now a creaking sound filled the air, along with a low, sleepy groan. Tom looked across the courtyard to see the mighty ogre, Okira, slowly unbend and lurch to his feet. He towered over the courtyard, a great hulk of a creature with a bald head, crooked nose and thick, rubbery lips.

As the Beast turned, Tom felt a sickening jolt of horror and Elenna gasped. Where the ogre's back should have been was another body – Kato's. Somehow it was enlarged,

and fused to Okira, making a
hideous two-headed Beast. The
Good Wizard stood out stiffly, as if
every muscle had seized up. His eyes

were white, like every Beast in the Isle of Ghosts, while his teeth were clenched together in a rictus of pain. Okira's eyes, too, had turned cloudy, while the dull grey stone of his body had morphed into leather-clad, moving flesh. Tom tightened his fist on his sword.

"Kato! Can you hear us?" Elenna called, but the wizard didn't stir.

Tom looked for Malvel, hoping to launch an attack, but his enemy had vanished. *Coward! Where is he?* Okira too scanned the courtyard, stopping when his blank eyes rested on Tom and Elenna.

"Okira!" Tom called, remembering how Kato and the ogre had been friends. "We're not your enemies. We're here to help." The ogre stared blankly at Tom, his brow creased with confusion. Tom felt a heartbeat of hope. But then the Beast's coarse features twisted with rage. He let out a furious roar, wrenching at the chain that bound him to the wall. The fastening came away, sending lumps of rock crashing to the ground.

The two-headed ogre charged towards Tom and Elenna, Kato bumping behind him, groaning in pain with each lumbering step. Tom took in the sheer size of the Beast and the thickness of the massive chain that he now brandished like a whip, and swallowed hard. The sword in Tom's hand looked like a toy compared to Okira – it would barely be a pin-prick in the creature's hide.

Elenna sent an arrow whizzing towards the ogre. It hit, sinking into his massive thigh. Okira bellowed with rage and plucked the arrow from his flesh as if it were no more than a thorn. He narrowed his eyes at Elenna, drew back his massive chain and lashed it towards her.

"Split up!" Elenna cried, darting away. Tom sprinted in the other direction, hugging the courtyard wall. A terrific crash rang out behind him and the ground shook beneath his feet. He glanced back to see Okira readying his whip once more. A huge crater had been smashed into the rock where Tom and Elenna had stood. Okira's whip whistled towards him, a blur of deadly steel. Tom called on the power of his golden boots and jumped the chain like it was a skipping rope, then ran on.

Crash! The mighty whip ploughed into the courtyard wall. Huge chunks of masonry clattered down. Tom lifted his shield to protect his head, feeling chips of rock glancing off his back and shoulders as he ran.

If that thing hits me, it'll break every bone in my body...

"Ha!" Malvel's laugh rang out above the din of falling stone and Tom glanced up to see the wizard grinning down at him from the summit of a tower. "You can't run for ever!" Malvel cried. "I'll steal the key to Avantia and when I return there, I'll make sure you're remembered as the foolish cowards you are!"

"Not on my watch!" Elenna cried. Tom looked back to see her standing before the keep, an arrow aimed up towards the wizard. But at the sound of her voice, Okira stopped in his tracks and turned, metal whip raised.

"Elenna! Watch out!" Tom shouted. Elenna spun to face the Beast, and let her arrow fly. It punched into the flesh of the monster's forearm. Okira bellowed in pain, then lurched across the courtyard in two vast strides. With the keep behind her, Elenna had nowhere to run. As she fumbled for another arrow, Tom leapt out after the Beast. Kato stared at Tom from Okira's back, the wizard's knuckles bloodless where they gripped his over-sized staff.

"Over here, you big brute!" Tom cried. Okira's ogre head spun to face him, white eyes burning. He brought his whip around in an arc, lashing it towards Tom. Calling on the power of his golden boots, Tom jumped, soaring upwards. The deadly chain

lashed beneath his feet and slammed
against the courtyard wall, sending
more stone flying. Tom landed in
a crouch. *Malvel's right about one
thing*, he thought. *I can't keep*

running. It's time to fight! He slung his shield over his back and sheathed his sword, fixing his eyes on Okira's massive chain as the ogre drew it back, then swung it at Tom's chest.

Tom focussed on the bright metal arcing towards him. He set his feet wide, waiting for just the right moment…

Now! Tom caught the end of the whip. The strain nearly pulled his arm from its sockets, but he managed to hang on, tugging the chain taut. His eyes were drawn to the middle of the chain. One of the links was gold, shining in the dim red light. *That must be the key that Malvel's after!* he realised.

With a grunt of effort, Tom gave the whip a mighty yank, trying to wrench it from the ogre's grip. Okira staggered forward, bent over, and Kato's body pulled him further off balance. The Beast fell to one knee and Tom felt a rush of hope. But then, with a grating roar, Okira clambered to his feet and heaved upwards on his chain. Tom's arms jerked above his head and his feet left the ground. With a sickening lurch, he was flying through the air. His grip slipped from the chain as the wind rushed past and the courtyard blurred. Stone brickwork loomed in front of him.

Crunch!

Tom cried out in agony as he slammed shoulder-first into the wall, slumping to the ground. He forced his eyes open and saw the blurry outline of Okira's broad shoulders and massive head filling his view. The ogre loomed over him, grinning horribly. Kato's face was a mask of pain and fear.

"Finish him!" Malvel cried. Okira let out a roar and brought his barrel-sized fist crashing down towards Tom. The hammer-like hand seemed to move in slow motion.

Tom thought of Avantia and the terrible suffering Malvel would unleash.

I've failed...

THE WIZARD'S STAFF

The fist slammed into the ground beside him. *He missed!* Tom realised, weak with relief. *But how?*

Okira let out a growl of pain, and Tom saw one of Elenna's arrows embedded in the ogre's meaty thumb. Tom scrambled to his feet to see Elenna with her back to the keep, another arrow already in her bow. He raced to her side.

Okira turned to face them, his whip hanging loosely in his injured fist and his face purple with rage. Over the ogre's massive shoulder, Tom could see Kato's hunched form. The wizard's eyes were screwed shut and every sinew stood out on his neck as he clenched his teeth.

"Kill him now!" Malvel's voice rang out from above. Okira lifted his hand to his mouth, yanked Elenna's arrow from his flesh with his teeth, then spat it to the ground. The ogre's lips spread in a gaptoothed grin and he lifted his chain once more.

Tom looked from Okira's hideous face to Kato's agonised grimace, his mind racing. They had to subdue the Beast – but how? And if they defeated Okira, would Kato survive? Then, to Tom's amazement, Kato stirred. His hunched body unbent and his milky eyes flickered, turning clear and sharp. His face contorted as if with a tremendous effort of will.

"Take my staff!" he hissed. "Aim where our bodies meet." Kato bent his arm and sent his massive staff spinning through the air, then slumped forwards again, his eyes fading to white.

Tom swallowed hard as the giant

wooden staff hurtled towards him, but he managed to catch it. It was twice his size. As soon as he wielded the staff, he felt it pulse with magical energy, shrinking in his grip. He aimed the staff at Okira, focussing on the point where

the ogre's flesh met that of the wizard. The staff seemed to jump in his hand and a bolt of red-hot fire shot from the tip. The sizzling energy struck Okira like lightning, tracing a searing red line between the ogre and the wizard before flaring so bright it filled the whole courtyard with light. When the brightness faded, Tom saw Okira stagger back, blinking as if in a daze. Kato lay on the cobbles before the ogre. The wizard stirred, shook his head, then rose shakily to his feet.

"No!" Malvel roared from his viewing point high on the tower. Tom and Elenna raced to Kato's side.

"Are you all right?" Elenna asked.

Sweat beaded the wizard's pale face, and his breath came in ragged gasps, but he nodded, his jaw set with grim determination. He reached for his staff.

"You take the Beast," Kato told Tom, nodding towards Okira. "Malvel is mine." Kato tapped the end of his staff on the ground, and vanished. Tom looked up to see him appear at the top of the tower near Malvel. The two wizards turned to face each other. With a fierce cry, Kato darted forwards, firing an orange energy bolt. Malvel threw up his own staff, releasing a blinding flash of purple. Tom had to look away, the light was so bright,

but he could hear crackles and booms echoing down from above as the two wizards duelled.

In the courtyard, Okira staggered about, colliding with walls and lashing his whip blindly. He looked mad with rage or pain.

"I'll distract him," said Elenna, darting out from the shadow of the keep, straight into the ogre's path.

"Over here!" she cried. Okira turned and narrowed his eyes, as if struggling to focus. Elenna waved, then set off at a run. The Beast lumbered after her, drawing his whip back over his shoulder ready to strike. Tom jumped out behind the ogre and grabbed the dangling end of the chain. Planting his feet wide, Tom heaved with all his strength. The ogre staggered backwards.

Tom sprang aside, then set off at a run, calling on the power of his leg armour. He circled the Beast with

magical speed, wrapping the end
of the metal chain about the ogre's
trunk-like legs. Okira swiped at
Tom with a meaty fist as Tom sped

past, but missed, throwing himself
further off balance. Tom raced on,
while Okira lifted his head and
howled in rage and confusion.
Finally, with the chain wound tight
about the ogre's legs, Tom nodded
to Elenna. She rushed to his side.

Together, they gave the end of the chain a mighty yank. Okira's arms windmilled in the air as he tried to catch himself, but it was no use. The Beast toppled like a tower hit with a battering ram.

Crack!

Okira's huge head slammed against the wall of the keep. His pale eyes flickered closed, and his body slumped on to the cobblestones.

Knocked out cold.

"We did it!" Elenna cried. But her smile suddenly changed to a look of alarm. "Kato!" she cried, staring in horror at the tower behind Tom. Tom spun to see a blue bolt of energy strike Kato square in the chest.

No!

The Good Wizard staggered back, stepped off the tower and plummeted. He landed in the courtyard with a hideous thump then lay as still as a pile of rags, his cloak tangled about him and his eyes closed.

THE QUEST
CONTINUES

Tom sprinted across the courtyard
with Elenna, looking up at the level
above. Malvel had vanished. Tom
sank to his knees at Kato's side,
searching the Good Wizard's face
for any sign of life. Elenna bent and
pressed her ear to Kato's chest.

"He's breathing!" she said. At

the sound of her voice, Kato's eyes flickered open. Tom fumbled for Epos's healing talon in his shield.

"Leave me!" Kato croaked. "You must finish this now. Malvel cannot succeed!"

"But you are wounded," Elenna cried. "You need help."

"Go!" Kato hissed. "I am trusting all to you. Do not let Malvel win!" Kato started to cough – weak, choking rasps that left him gasping for breath. Tom met Elenna's anguished gaze.

"We have to do as he says," he told her.

"Ha! Too late for that," a sneering voice cried. Tom looked up from

the injured wizard to see Malvel
now standing at Okira's feet. A
small gold chain link glinted in the
wizard's hand.

The key! Tom realised with a lurch
of dread.

"While you were busy playing
nursemaid, I have taken what I
came for," Malvel went on. "I will
use this key to return to Avantia.
Hugo's throne will be mine!"

"Never!" Tom cried, leaping to
his feet. He lifted his sword and
tore across the courtyard towards
the Dark Wizard. Malvel smiled
and lifted his staff. *Crack!* A bolt of
purple energy fizzed towards Tom.
He threw up his shield. *BOOF!* He

found himself hurtling backwards through the air. He landed hard on the rough ground and skidded.

"Tom!" Elenna cried. Tom looked and saw her pointing up to the top of the courtyard wall. Malvel had transported himself and stood there gazing down at them with a triumphant smile. In one hand he held the golden link, and in the other the Amulet of Avantia.

"Goodbye, Tom!" Malvel cried. "It's almost a shame I won't be here to see you rot!" Despair crashed over Tom like a tidal wave, leaving him weak and sick. There was no way he could stop Malvel now. He'd lost. He'd failed and all of Avantia

would suffer. But as Malvel drew
the golden link towards the amulet
with a theatrical flourish, Okira
stirred. The Beast let out a bellow
of rage and drove his massive

fist through the courtyard wall, right below where Malvel stood. The wizard's smile vanished. He stumbled forwards, the brickwork crumbling beneath his feet. Tom saw the golden link drop from Malvel's hand, glinting as it spun through the air.

Elenna raced towards the falling link. "Got it!" she cried, snatching it from the air. But with a flash of purple, a dark figure appeared behind her.

Malvel! "Watch out!" Tom cried, too late. Malvel grabbed Elenna roughly and placed a knife against her throat.

"Give me the key," Malvel hissed.

"Never!" Elenna said. But Tom saw her eyes widen in pain as Malvel pressed the blade hard against her skin.

"Then I'll take it from your lifeless

body," Malvel snarled.

"Give him the link!" Tom cried in panic.

Elenna closed her eyes for a moment, as if saying a silent prayer, then slowly lifted her hand. She opened her fist to reveal the golden link. But before Malvel could take it, Elenna whipped back her arm and cast the link from her, sending it spinning through the hole Okira had smashed in the courtyard wall.

Tom heard the link land in the acid moat with a *plop*. As Malvel let out a howl of rage, Elenna grabbed the arm at her throat with both hands and yanked it downwards and away from her. Then she stuck

out her leg and twisted her body,
flipping Malvel over her hip to
land on the ground in a tangle of
robes. Elenna stepped back and
grabbed her bow, aiming an arrow
at Malvel's chest. The Dark Wizard
gritted his teeth.

"This isn't over!" he hissed, then vanished.

Elenna let her bow fall.

Tom found himself staring at his friend in awe, but before he could congratulate her, he heard a ragged cough from behind him. Tom turned

to see Kato trying to sit up. The
wizard fell back, gasping with pain.

"I knew you would succeed," Kato
wheezed. Tom walked to his side
and Elenna joined him. They both
crouched beside the wizard. Tom
supported Kato's head. From the

other side of the courtyard, Okira watched them with a mournful gaze. The Beast had returned to his huddled crouch, hugging his knees, like a scolded child. Tom put his hand to the red jewel in his belt and at once felt a wave of remorse and shame from the Beast.

"Don't blame yourself for what happened," he told Okira. "You were acting under Malvel's power. Malvel alone is responsible, and Malvel alone shall pay."

Tom felt Kato's hand tighten on his arm. "I don't have long," the wizard said, his voice little more than a whisper. "But before I go, there are things you must know."

"No!" Tom started to protest. "I can heal you!" But Kato clutched his arm tighter and went on, his feverish eyes locked with Tom's.

"Only through death can I escape this place," Kato said. "But you and Elenna can still be free. There is only one more key in the Isle of Ghosts. You must defeat the Beast that guards it – a Beast loyal to Malvel. If you do not, all is lost. You and Elenna will become spirits, trapped in this land for ever."

Tom stared into Kato's face as the Gorgonian wizard's eyes closed and his body went still. *He's dead.*

Sorrow and fury raged inside Tom. "I promise you," he vowed at last, his voice husky with grief, "while there's blood in my veins, Malvel will never leave this place."

THE END

CONGRATULATIONS, YOU HAVE COMPLETED THIS QUEST!

At the end of each chapter you were awarded a special gold coin.
The QUEST in this book was worth an amazing 8 coins.

Look at the Beast Quest totem picture inside the back cover of this book to see how far you've come in your journey to become

MASTER OF THE BEASTS.

The more books you read, the more coins you will collect!

Do you want your own
Beast Quest Totem?

1. Cut out and collect the coin below
2. Go to the Beast Quest website
3. Download and print out your totem
4. Add your coin to the totem
www.beastquest.co.uk/totem

*Don't miss the next
exciting Beast Quest
book, RYKAR THE
FIRE HOUND!*

*Read on for a sneak
peek...*

TO THE SHARD
MOUNTAINS

Kato's body felt cold and heavy in
Tom's arms.

A breeze stirred the old man's
long white beard, as Tom laid him
down gently on the flagstones. He
remembered the sneering face of

Malvel. How the Dark Wizard had slain Kato, then fled like a coward. Tom made a silent promise. *You won't go unavenged...*

"Is he...?" asked Elenna.

Tom nodded. "It's over."

As he said the words, the wizard's body began to twinkle with golden speckles of light. Then, slowly, it vanished into nothing. Only Kato's wooden staff was left.

Tom got to his feet, surveying the grey stone courtyard. Elenna stood nearby with Okira. The ogre towered five times as tall as Tom, with muscles like rocks and a head as big as a boulder. But as he knelt down beside Kato's staff, he looked like a lost, frightened child.

"This is not your fault," Tom said
to the ogre. *There's only one person*

to blame for this...

He turned to Elenna. "We have to get to the Shard Mountains. Kato said that Malvel would be heading that way. We have to stop him leaving the Isle of Ghosts."

The ogre shook his massive head. His voice rumbled like thunder in Tom's mind.

There is a dark and deadly Beast that lurks in the Shard Mountains... Malvel holds sway over him.

Tom nodded, feeling a squirm of unease. The Dark Wizard had stolen his father's amulet, the link between the spirit world and the world of the living. All Malvel needed was for this new Beast to give up his magical key.

Then he'll use it to escape the Isle of Ghosts and leave us stranded here for ever...

"We'll need to cross the moat first," Tom said, gazing over towards the smashed drawbridge.

"The one that's full of acid?" asked Elenna, with an arched eyebrow.

"I didn't say it would be easy." Tom picked his way through fallen rubble to a gaping hole in the courtyard wall that Okira had made with his fists. Through it, he could see the moat seething and bubbling. Elenna came to join him. "Maybe I could carry you?" Tom suggested. "If I use the power of the golden boots, I might be able to jump across."

Elenna shook her head. "I don't know, Tom... It's a long way, even without me on your back."

Without speaking, Okira strode to one of the guard towers set in the courtyard walls. He turned and pressed his back against the base of the tower. Then with a growl he began to push, muscles bulging.

"Rrrrrrraaaargh!"

Tom felt the stones of the courtyard shake beneath his feet. The tower groaned and shuddered. Suddenly it gave way, collapsing into the moat with a deafening clashing of rocks. Plumes of acid splattered all around. Tom flung up his shield to protect himself and Elenna, and

he heard a sizzle as some liquid
splashed against it.

When the crashing died away, Tom

lowered his shield. The tower lay half submerged in the moat, forming a bridge across it. The acid hissed and fizzed at the stone, but didn't seem to damage it at all.

The stone is from the Shard Mountains, rumbled Okira, wiping sweat from his brow. *It cannot be melted. Except by Rykar, so it is said.*

Tom placed his fingers against the red jewel in his belt, to speak to the ogre. *Who is Rykar?*

The Beast you seek to battle, said Okira. *Come. I will guide you.* He clambered up on to the wall of the fallen tower and pointed towards a cluster of dark peaks on the horizon. *That is where you must travel. The*

Shard Mountains!

Tom and Elenna followed Okira along a worn track, across a barren, rocky plain. After half a day's travelling, they had left Kato's Castle far behind. In the distance, the mountains rose up like giant black teeth jutting crookedly into the gloomy sky.

The ogre frowned, and his voice rumbled with anger. *I have trodden this path many times. Malvel made me carry rocks from the mountains to rebuild the castle.*

When will we get there? asked Tom.

Soon – we must be patient, Okira

replied. Suddenly, the ogre stumbled to a halt, groaning and clutching at his head.

"What's wrong?" asked Elenna, drawing her bow.

Tom's hand closed on his sword hilt. He looked all around, but they were alone.

Evil magic, grunted Okira. *I can feel it! There is some enchantment on the road.*

"Is there some way past it?" said Tom.

Okira shook his head. *I can go no further*, he said. *I must return to the castle. It is my duty to guard it. Farewell, Master of the Beasts, and be careful.* Backing away, he raised a

hand in farewell.

"Goodbye, Okira," Elenna said.

"And thank you," Tom added.

They watched the ogre turn and plod away, back to his lonely fortress home. Then they set off again towards the mountains.

The day wore on, and a chill wind began to blow across the plain. It howled mournfully, making Tom and Elenna shiver.

"What's that up ahead?" asked Elenna suddenly.

Tom peered into the distance. His heart hammered as he spotted a hooded figure on the road, heading towards them. Tom drew his sword and shield. "Be ready," he said.

Read
RYKAR THE FIRE HOUND
to find out what happens next!

Beast Quest

AVAILABLE AUTUMN 2017

The epic adventure is brought to life on **Xbox One** and **PS4** for the first time ever!

www.maximumgames.com   www.beast-quest.com